Little Raccoon

SCHOLASTIC INC

and the Outside World

by LILIAN MOORE • Pictures by GIOIA FIAMMENGHI

New York Toronto London Auckland Sydney

ISBN 0-590-42593-5

12 11 10 9 8 7 6 5 4 3 2 1   9/8 0 1 2 3/9

Printed in the U.S.A.   23

*For Mary Bressler Wolman —
who understands about things
that are hard to explain*

Little Raccoon looked out
at the woods around him.

There was nothing
to see but the woods.
Nothing but green woodland
all around.

Little Raccoon sat thinking.

"Mother," he asked.
"Do the woods have an end?
Do they go on and on —
or do they end?"

"The woods have an end,"
said his mother.
"Past the running stream,
past the bright berry bushes,
past the open grass
where the young oak stands —
the woods end."

"But what is there —
after the woods end?"
asked Little Raccoon.

"The outside world,"
said Mother Raccoon.

"The outside world!"
cried Little Raccoon.
"What is it like?"

"It's too hard to explain,"
said his mother.
"Why don't you run out and play?"

Little Raccoon ran out,
but he did not play.
He sat down to think.

Mother Skunk came by
with her little ones.
Little Raccoon jumped up
and ran to her.

"Please!" he said.
"What is it like
in the outside world?"

"Way out there?" said Mother Skunk.
"Past the running stream,
past the bright berry bushes,
past the open grass
where the young oak stands?"

"Yes! Yes!" cried Little Raccoon.

"It's too hard to explain,"
said Mother Skunk.
And she went in to visit
with Mother Raccoon.

The little skunks wanted to play,
but Little Raccoon wanted to think.
So the little skunks sat down to think, too.

"If I go to the running stream,"
said Little Raccoon,
"I can catch a crayfish.
I can stand on a big rock.
And maybe I can *see* the outside world!"

"Oh good!" cried the skunks.
"We will go too.
Maybe we can catch a frog!"

Little Raccoon looked at the skunks.
"Well, come along," he said.
"But stay right behind me,
and do as I say."

Off they went to the running stream,
and the little skunks stayed
right behind Little Raccoon,
all the way.

Little Raccoon looked for a crayfish.
The little skunks looked for a frog.
They saw a frog and they ran after it.

But the little skunks bumped heads,
and the frog got away.

Little Raccoon did catch a crayfish.

Then he got up on a big rock.

But he did not see the outside world.

"If I go on to the berry bushes,"
said Little Raccoon,
"I can eat some berries.
I can climb a tall bush.
And maybe then I can see the outside world."

"We *love* berries!" said the skunks.

"Well, come along then,"
said Little Raccoon.
"But stay right behind me,
and do as I say."

Off they went to the berry bushes,
and the little skunks stayed
right behind Little Raccoon.

They ate and ate the fat bright berries.

One more.

And one more.

And one more.

Then Little Raccoon climbed a tall bush.
But he did not see the outside world.

"If I go on to the open grass," he said,
"I can catch some bugs and creeping things.
I can climb the young oak tree.
Maybe then I can see the outside world."

"We just *love* bugs and creeping things!"
cried the little skunks.

"Come along," said Little Raccoon,
and on they went to the open grass.

They ran after bugs
and creeping things.

And they ate and ate.

Then Little Raccoon climbed up
the young oak tree.

And he *did* see something!

"That's it!" cried Little Raccoon.
"That must be the outside world!"

"What is it? What is it like?"
asked the skunks.

"I am going to find out,"
said Little Raccoon.

"Oh good!" cried the skunks.
"We will go too!"

This time Little Raccoon said no.

"You are too little," he said.

"You stay here.

I will come back and tell you."

Little Raccoon ran across the open grass
to the end of the woods.

What was this?

He stopped and looked.

Then he ran inside.

What was this?
Maybe it was like the tree
over the pool in the woods.
Maybe it was something to run across.

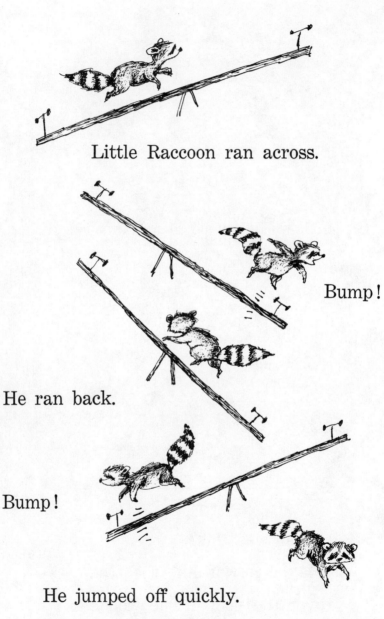

Little Raccoon ran across.

Bump!

He ran back.

Bump!

He jumped off quickly.
It was *not* like the tree over the pool.

Then Little Raccoon smelled something.
All good things were mixed up
into that one good smell.

Sniff! Sniff!
It came from here.

Little Raccoon looked inside.
So many good things!

One thing was best of all.

But it *was* a little hard to eat.

Little Raccoon ran back
to the skunks.

He ran back to tell them
—about the thing that went bump,
—and the good smell,
—and the long, long, *long* things to eat.

"You stay right here,"
said Little Raccoon.
"I will come back and tell you more."

Little Raccoon ran across the grass again.

What was this?

It must be a tree.

But what BIG leaves it had!

It was hard to climb, too.

Little Raccoon ran to the fence.
Then he jumped from the fence
to the tree.

The tree began to go around!

Little Raccoon wanted to get off.
He jumped again, and there he was,
sitting right in one of the BIG leaves!

At last Little Raccoon got off.
He ran back to the skunks to tell them
about the trees in the outside world.

"They have big, big leaves,"
said Little Raccoon, "and guess what!"
The trees go around and around!"

"We will stay right here,"
said the little skunks quickly.
"You can come back and
tell us more."

Again Little Raccoon
ran across the grass
to the end of the woods.

Again he looked around.

What was this?
What was down *there?*
Little Raccoon ran down to see.

There was something to open.

Little Raccoon opened it.

There was something to climb.

Little Raccoon climbed it.

There was something to pull.
Little Raccoon pulled it.

Whoosh!
Down came the water.
Cold water.
Then warm water.
Then HOT water.

"OW!" cried Little Raccoon,
and he jumped out quickly.

Little Raccoon ran all the way back
to the little skunks.

"Guess what!" he cried.
"The outside world is where
they keep the rain!
I turned on the rain!
And guess what—
it was HOT rain!"

"HOT rain!" cried the little skunks.
"We want to go home!"

So did Little Raccoon.
He had so *many* things
to tell his mother.

"Come along!"
he cried to the little skunks.

They ran back across the open grass.
And they did not stop
for one little bug.

They ran past the berry bushes.
And they did not stop
for one fat bright berry.

They ran past the running stream.
And they did not stop
to look for a crayfish or a frog.

They ran all the way back—
all the way to Little Raccoon's house.

Mother Skunk was still visiting
with Mother Raccoon.

"Guess what!" cried the little skunks.
"We went all the way to the open grass,
and Little Raccoon went to see
the outside world!"

"The outside world!" said Mother Skunk.
"Think of that!"

"Did you really?" said Mother Raccoon.
"What was it like, Little Raccoon?"

What was it like?

Little Raccoon began to think
—about things that went *bump*
—about long, *long* things to eat,
—about trees that went around,
—about rain that was HOT.

"It's too hard to explain,"
said Little Raccoon.